Arena-Taschenbuch
Band 2850

KNISTER

geboren 1952, lebt in Wesel.
KNISTER schreibt Bücher,
macht Musikkassetten und CD-ROM.
Verrückt, lustig und spannend. Immer!
Lieblingsfarbe: BUNT.
Lieblingsessen: Spagetti zu jeder Tageszeit.
Hobby: In einer Rockband spielen
Sternzeichen: Frosch

Ellen Butzko,

geboren 1963, ist Englischlehrerin an einem Gymnasium, als Fachleiterin auch in der Referendarausbildung tätig und Mitglied einer Arbeitsgruppe zur Grundschuldidaktik.

Birgit Rieger

lebt und arbeitet in Berlin. Als freischaffende Grafikerin gestaltet und illustriert sie Bücher für Kinder und Jugendliche.

KNISTER

Lilli the Witch
Trouble at School

Englische Textfassung von
Ellen Butzko

Mit Illustrationen von
Birgit Rieger

Arena

1. Auflage dieser Ausgabe als Arena-Taschenbuch 2003

Englische Fassung: Ellen Butzko

Umschlaggestaltung und Innenillustrationen: Birgit Rieger
Gesamtherstellung: Westermann Druck Zwickau GmbH
ISSN 0518-4002
ISBN 3-401-02850-2

Magic words

witch – Hexe
witchcraft – Zauberei
practical joke – Streich
tricks of witchcraft – Hexentricks
magic – Zauberei
magic broom – Zauberbesen
magic spell – Zauberspruch
fireworks – Feuerwerk
turn/turn into – verwandeln, sich verwandeln
secret – geheim
careful – vorsichtig
quiet/quietly – leise
strange – seltsam
surprise – Überraschung
it works – es funktioniert
trip – stolpern
by chance – zufällig
chance – Zufall

Lilli the Witch: Trouble at School

This is Lilli.
She's your age
and looks like
a normal child.
She *is* a normal
child, but . . .
not really. Lilli has a book.
This is *not* a normal book:
it's a book of witchcraft.
One morning Lilli looks under her bed –
and surprise, surprise:
there it is, the book of witchcraft!
Lilli has no idea who put it there.
But she knows that
the book is full of real magic
and wild tricks of witchcraft.
Lilli can do some of these tricks.
But careful!

If *you* do these tricks,
it can be very dangerous:
one wrong word and –
a magic broom turns into a skateboard,
a teacher turns into a penguin,
ice-cream turns into a schnitzel.
That's why nobody knows
that Lilli has this book.
That's why nobody knows
that she's a secret witch.
And that's why Leon doesn't know
that she can do magic tricks.
Who's Leon?
He's Lilli's little brother.
Leon asks lots of questions.
Little brothers can really
get on your nerves!
But Lilli also loves her
little brother very much . . .

Let's start with our story then.

schnitzel – Schnitzel (das gibt es tatsächlich in Amerika so!)
can get on your nerves – kann dir auf die Nerven gehen

Chapter 1

"Lilli, Lilli, I must tell you something!"

Oh no, it's Leon!

He's getting on Lilli's nerves again.

It's Tuesday afternoon.

School is over.

Leon was there with his mother today.

He was there to register

for the first school year.

to register – um sich anzumelden

Leon is so happy now.
He must tell Lilli how good
his first day was at school.
"Lilli, Lilli, where are you?
I must tell you something."
Lilli wants to be alone.
She's under her bed
but Leon finds her there.
"Lilli, Lilli, I was at school
for an interview with the headmaster,"
Leon says.
"Imagine Lilli, he asked me two
questions.
He asked me where's left?
and where's right?
and – of course I knew the answer!"

headmaster – Schulleiter
of course – natürlich
I knew – ich wusste

Lilli says: "Of course you know the answer to these two questions!"
Leon is very proud. He says:
"Well, . . . just one little mistake . . ."
Lilli answers: "Wonderful,
only one mistake with left and right.
That's what I call clever."
Lilli's mother stands in the door now.
Lilli winks at her.
Leon says: "Well, I'm a big pupil now."
"You just wait!" mother says. "School can be hard."
"You just wait! Lilli says. "School is not what you think."
"You just wait!" Leon says. "School will be super!"

proud – stolz
winks – zwinkert
pupil – Schüler
will – wird

Mother walks back
into the living-room. Leon can't leave
Lilli alone. He wants to find out
more about school.
"What about you? Nice day at school?"
Leon talks like a really big pupil now.
Lilli answers: "Just a normal day."
Leon wants to know:
"Well, what's normal for you?"
Lilli is fed up: "Just normal,
reading and writing and . . ."
but then Lilli remembers:
". . . but tomorrow something special
is going to happen.
An inspector is going to come
to our school tomorrow.

is fed up – hat die Nase voll
remembers – erinnert sich
is going to happen – wird passieren

He's going to sit in our class
and watch our teacher."
Leon doesn't understand.
"And why?"
Lilli tells him: "He wants to check
on Ms Howard, our teacher."
Leon understands:
"Ah, so he's like a policeman
for teachers, this inspector?"
"Yes, something like that,"
Lilli answers. "He checks on teachers.
He wants to see
that they do a good job.

And tomorrow he's going
to check on Ms Howard."
Now Leon really understands
everything: "Oh, he's
like a sheriff then.
He walks through town.
And when he sees a bad man –
BANG, BANG, BANG!"
"No, Leon, *that* is not going to happen
tomorrow," Lilli laughs. "I don't think
he has a revolver!
He just wants to see
that we learn the right things
from Ms Howard.
Ms Howard says
we must be very nice tomorrow
and very polite."
"Polite??? What's that?" Leon asks.
"You're polite, for example,

if you don't forget to say PLEASE.
Or if you say ›sir‹, not ›uncle‹
to a man that you don't know.
Or . . ."
"Or if I give my seat on the bus
to mother's friend
so she can sit down.
Or if somebody farts
and it stinks like in the zoo
and I think I'm going to die
but I'm polite and I just say:
›Don't worry, I can't smell a thing!‹"
Lilli giggles: "Yes, you're right,
that's polite. You *are* a clever boy!
And now you can be a clever pupil
and leave me alone

seat – Sitzplatz
farts – furzt
giggles – kichert

so I can do my homework."
Leon is happy now.
He takes one of Lilli's comics
and goes out of the room.
Lilli is alone. ☆
She closes the door.
Then she gets a chair . . .

Nobody can come in now.
Why does she do that?
Simple: Lilli must be alone
because she wants to do secret magic.
She has a brilliant idea.
An idea for tomorrow . . .

Chapter 2

Lilli finds her magic book of witchcraft under her bed. Then she gets a pencil and a piece of paper.
Now she can write down her ideas.

"Let's see," Lilli says.
She goes through her magic book.
All these wonderful magic tricks!
The book is in alphabetical order.
Under B she finds
something about BROOMS,

under F she finds
something about FIREWORKS,
and then under H
she finds HURLY-BURLY.
What a strange word!
Lilli has no idea what it means.
Maybe it's black magic?
Lilli doesn't want to know
more about it. She knows
that she must be very careful
with this magic book.
OOPS, what's this?
She reads and reads
but she doesn't see and
she doesn't feel that
her hair suddenly stands on end!
It looks wild.

her hair suddenly stands on end – die Haare stehen ihr plötzlich zu Berge

But Lilli reads on and on.
Maybe it has something to do with
that strange word HURLY-BURLY.
Suddenly her hair turns black.
Then it turns blue,
blue like the ocean.
It's only for a moment.
Then it's over again.
"Ah, here it is," Lilli says.
This is her plan:
Lilli wants to help Ms Howard
so that the inspector
will give her an A+.
But Lilli needs special tricks
for this plan. She finds ideas
here and there in her magic book.
She writes them all down.

A+ – eine Eins in der Schule
(übrigens: ein F ist eine Sechs)

When she's done,
she closes the book very carefully
and puts it back under her bed.
Then she sits down at her desk
and looks at the piece of paper.
She giggles as she reads
her ideas again.
There are seven or eight magic spells
on the page.
She will try them out tomorrow.
And the inspector
will be very surprised . . .
There's just one little problem.
Lilli can't take
the magic book to school.
First, because it's very heavy.

she's done – sie ist fertig
try out – ausprobieren
heavy – schwer

Second, because it's a secret book.
So she must say these magic spells
over and over again.
The tricks must be perfect
for school tomorrow.
Lilli knows that she can't say
these magic spells out loud.
They can be very dangerous!
So she reads
these strange words silently.
She hopes that she will learn them
like that.
But it's not easy!
After half an hour
her head is spinning . . .

silently – still
her head is spinning – ihr raucht der Kopf

Chapter 3

It's the next morning.
Lilli can't wait to be at school!
Her plan is perfect now:
she has a piece of paper
with her magic spells
in her pocket.

In the classroom
the teacher tells the children
that the inspector will come
in the next five or ten minutes.
"Please be good and please be polite,"

Ms Howard says again.
"And please pay attention.
Then nothing can go wrong."
The children are nervous now.
Lilli is quite cool:
"Nothing will go wrong!"
She really wants to tell Ms Howard
about her plan.
She knows that
(with a little bit of magic)
everything will be fine.
But a secret witch
can't tell a single person
about her magic tricks!
One of Lilli's friends, Basti, asks:
"What's he like, this inspector?"
Ms Howard answers:
"I don't know him
but the others say he . . ."

There's a knock at the door.
"That's him!" All the children
turn their heads and look at the door.
Lilli is the only one
who can't look at the door
because she takes out
her little piece of paper
with the magic spells.
Then she reads the words.

One of the girls goes to the door.
Lilli says some words

knock – Klopfen

but nobody hears her.
The door opens and . . .
no, it's not the inspector,
it's the school secretary, Mrs Berry.
She has some papers for Ms Howard.
"This is for you, Ms Howard,
so that you can . . ."

This is all that she can say
because suddenly she trips
and lands face down on the floor.
Ms Howard runs to her.
She wants to help her to get up.
Ten children run to her.
They want to help her, too.
But Mrs Berry is up already

face down – mit dem Gesicht nach unten

and only says:
"You're *really* polite children."
Ms Howard is still worried:
"Are you sure you're all right?"
Mrs Berry says: "Absolutely sure.
But I just don't know
how that could happen."
Well, Lilli knows
how that could happen.
She doesn't say a word. She smiles.
She's happy that the trick
with the tripping
worked perfectly.
Well, not exactly perfectly
because the plan was
that the inspector should trip
and not the secretary. But now

how that could happen – wie das passieren konnte

they all know that the class
can be polite. And Lilli knows
that her magic trick works.
There are still many children
at the front of the classroom,
when the door opens again.
A man suddenly stands in the room.
"My name is Stuart,
Mr Michael Stuart," he shouts.
"Is this Ms Howard's class?"
"Yes, yes, I'm Ms Howard.
I'm so sorry. We have a little bit
of a chaos here, as you can see."
"Oh yes, I can see that."
Then Mr Stuart goes on:
"I don't normally come in like this.
But there was nobody

shout – rufen

in the secretary's room.
I asked another pupil
and he showed me this room.
I knocked at the door
but nobody opened it and so . . ."
The secretary says:
"There's always somebody
in the secretary's room."
She knows that this man
can only be the inspector.
And she knows
that she wasn't in her room.

So she must say something
to explain the situation.
"I was only out
for two or three minutes
to bring Ms Howard some papers."
Then one boy says:
"And we normally hear
when somebody knocks at the door."
Another boy shouts: "There was just
a little bit of a chaos here."
A third boy yells: "And we always
open the door, especially for
inspectors and headmasters!"
And a fourth child is louder
than all three together:
"Because we're
really polite children."

to explain – erklären
yell – brüllen

The inspector asks:

"Are you always like this?

Don't you ever put up your hands

when you want to say something?"

Ms Howard explains:

"The children are excited

that you're here.

This is not a normal situation.

And then Mrs Berry tripped."

Lilli thinks: OUCH! This is not

what I wanted.

I must do something fast.

The inspector doesn't look very happy.

Lilli takes out her piece of paper again.

But this time the spell is too strong:

WHOOPS! Half the class,

plus the inspector, the secretary,

Don't you ever put up your hands . . .? – Meldet ihr euch nie . . .?

and the teacher fall down.
Now the rest of the class
run to the others
to help them get up!
There's complete chaos now.
Lilli is totally shocked.
She sits at her desk
and watches the others.
Slowly the situation goes back
to normal again.
The children go back to their desks.

Mrs Berry gets up.

She says good-bye.

Then it turns quiet in the classroom.

Very quiet. Extremely quiet.

Ms Howard says:

"Okay . . . let's begin then."

And the inspector says:

"Never, I have never

in my whole life . . ."

and he writes many, many things

in his little black book.

Ms Howard goes down on her knees
and checks the floor.
"I just don't know.
Maybe the janitor
put too much polish on the floor.
Maybe he wanted to make the room
perfect for you."
The inspector writes and writes.
"Never, I have never
in my whole life . . .
I must tell the school board
about this."
Lilli thinks OUCH! again.
What does the inspector write
in his little black book?

knees – Knie
janitor – Hausmeister
polish – Bohnerwachs
school board – Schulamt

Can it be positive?
It's not the teacher's fault
when people trip by chance.
By chance . . .
Lilli knows it wasn't by chance.
The spell for tripping
is on her piece of paper, too.
Lilli looks at her spells again.
There's one spell for smoke.
It's only an emergency spell –
but is this not an emergency now?
Lilli says some words quietly.

smoke – Rauch
emergency – Notfall, für Notfälle

Moments later the alarm goes off.
Fire alarm!
"What's this now?"
The inspector looks at Ms Howard.
She says: "I don't think it's a fire.
It can only be a fire drill.
I'm sure it's only a fire drill."
The inspector looks through his book.
"Today? I don't know anything
about a fire drill. Why don't they
tell me about these things?"
Ms Howard says:
"Maybe it's something serious.
You never know."
The inspector doesn't think so.
"Nonsense! I'm sure

fire drill – Feuerwehrübung
serious – ernst
nonsense – Blödsinn

it's only a practical joke. When I
was a pupil, we always
did something . . . I mean,
we *never* did anything like that!"
Ms Howard isn't so sure.
"But maybe this is a real alarm now."
The inspector doesn't want to hear
more about this. "Please begin
your lesson now."
Smoke is coming into the classroom
from under the door.
All the children cry out in panic
and the inspector turns white
in the face.
"Get out everybody! Get out now!"
He runs to the door.
But Ms Howard blocks the door.

practical joke – Streich

"You can't open the door," she shouts, "that is where the smoke is coming from!"
Mr Stuart is very hectic now: "Then open the windows or we will all die."
Ms Howard shakes her head. "The windows must be closed when there's a fire."
She goes over to the window and stands right in front of it.
"The rules say that you shouldn't open the windows. If we let in fresh air, the fire can grow bigger."
Mr Stuart says: "You're right,

shakes her head – schüttelt den Kopf
fresh air – frische Luft

you're absolutely right. I mean
I know that the windows
must be closed but I think
I was so shocked that I forgot."
He's totally white in the face now.
One child asks: "But what
are we going to do?"
Ms Howard is very calm:
"We must wait. But we can
do something about the smoke."

calm – ruhig

She takes off her jacket, rolls it up
and puts it under the door.
The smoke can't get through now.
Other children bring their jackets.
One girl wants to take off her pullover.
But Ms Howard doesn't let her.
"That's fine.
Please everybody sit down.
We're going to wait and see."
Suddenly Ms Howard smiles.
"Maybe this is the janitor's idea!
Maybe he's blowing cigarette smoke
through the door.
He just wants to test us
because the inspector is here.
Or maybe this is your idea,
Mr Stuart. You want to test us!"

he's blowing – er bläst

The inspector
still doesn't look very happy.
"I can't tell you, Ms Howard.
But you're doing fine,
that's all I can say."
"Look, look, look!"
Twenty children run to the window.
Everybody can hear it now: a siren.
The fire brigade is here
with three vehicles.
Not long after that
somebody knocks at the door.
A fireman with a helmet
and heavy boots
tells the children to come out.

fire brigade – Feuerwehr
vehicle – Fahrzeug
fireman – Feuerwehrmann
helmet – Helm
boot – Stiefel

"Take each other by the hand
and come with me."
The rest is easy:
the children make a long line.
The inspector is at the end
(now only his nose is white).
Everybody leaves the classroom.
YUK, that smell! Lilli is glad
that she's in the playground.

yuk – igitt

All the other children are glad, too.
It's good to be out in the open.
Other classes
are in the playground, too.
Chaos at school . . .
What's the problem?
Somewhere there must be a fire.
Or is there a fire at all?
There's smoke,

at all – überhaupt

but nobody can see flames.

Can there be smoke without fire???

The firemen roll out hoses

and run back and forth.

They try to find the fire.

But after 15 minutes they give up.

There's no fire. Nobody has a clue.

flame – Flamme
hose – Schlauch
nobody has a clue – keiner blickt durch

Nobody? Lilli the witch has a clue.
The spell is over
but it takes some time
until the smoke is gone.
And after the smoke is gone,
the fire brigade is gone, too.
The children and the teachers
can go back to their classrooms now.

Chapter 4

The inspector is back in his chair.
(His nose is back to its normal colour.)
"Let's start, Ms Howard.
There's not much time left."
His little black book
is back on his desk.
He looks grim.
OUCH! Lilli is worried.
Her idea with the emergency spell
was not very good.
What can she do now?
She looks at her piece of paper.
Ah, she has this spell for LOVE!
Lilli's idea was
that the inspector should be
nice to Ms Howard
but there was no spell in her book

left – übrig
grim – grimmig

for NICE. Lilli then remembered
what her mother always says
when she wants to be nice.
"That's lovely, dear."
Too bad that there was
nothing under DEAR and
nothing under LOVELY.
But Lilli never gives up easily.
There was a spell for LOVE
in her book. That's practically
the same as nice, isn't it?
At the moment the inspector
doesn't look very nice.
And this is all Lilli's fault!
It's because of Lilli
that there's trouble at school!
Should she say the spell now?
It could go wrong again.
It's all right, Lilli thinks,

the situation can't get more chaotic
than it is now.
And that's why she says
the tricky spell for LOVE.

Seconds later
the inspector looks no longer grim.
His eyes are shining now
as he looks at the children
and at the teacher.
"Ah, Ms Howard," he smiles,
"I look at you and I must say
I'm quite fond of you."
"Sorry . . . what are you saying?"
Ms Howard doesn't have a clue
what he wants to tell her.

His eyes are shining – Seine Augen leuchten
I'm quite fond of you – ich mag Sie sehr

The inspector says: "I mean,
I feel so strange. It's . . . I feel . . .
This is so funny . . .
I can't understand . . . I mean . . .
I'm not married. Are you . . . well . . .
are you married?"
Oh no! Not again!
Lilli can see
that this was the wrong spell again!
She says her spell once more,
this time very fast.

married – verheiratet

She wants to take back the magic.
This works perfectly.
The inspector's eyes
aren't shining any more.
But Lilli's class-mates
now give each other hugs and kisses!
This is a big surprise
for Mr Stuart and Ms Howard.
They just sit and watch.
Lilli thinks: I must do something!
She says her spell for LOVE again.

She hopes that she can say
these tricky words correctly.

hug – Umarmung

She sits and waits.
Steven and Sabrina –
normally they're not best friends.
And now they're holding hands!
But wait, something is happening:
Sabrina gets up and shouts at Steven.
"What are you doing, you twit!
Go away and leave me alone."

twit – Dummkopf

Lilli thinks: great. Wonderful.
That's it. The spell is over.
They're all back to normal.
Not all, some are suddenly very nasty.
Peter (he sits behind Lilli) gets up
and says: "This really stinks,
Ms Howard."
All the children look at Peter.

nasty – gemein

They're shocked.
Ms Howard only says: "Well, Peter.
You say it stinks.
I say we need some fresh air."
And she goes to the window
and opens it.
The inspector is busy
with his little black book.
He doesn't hear what goes on
in the classroom.
Now he looks up and says:
"Ms Howard, let's start
with a normal lesson. Please."
Ms Howard must do
what the inspector says.
She goes back to her desk
and looks into her bag.
She takes out five apples,
beautiful red apples.

She takes two apples in one hand
and three apples in the other hand.
Then she asks the class:
"I have two apples in my left hand
and three apples in my right hand.
What's that?"
Lilli shouts as loud as she can: "Five!"
Oh no! How can she do that!
She must always
put up her hand first!
Lilli is worried
that she always does the wrong thing.
But she really
wants to help her teacher.
Ms Howard says: "Five, that's correct.
But there's a second correct answer."
Lilli doesn't have a clue.
Ms Howard wants to help her:
"That's easy, think about it!"

Lars shouts: "That's not fair.
What Lilli says is correct.
Two and three is five!"
Ms Howard says: "Correct.
But there's a second answer."
Lars asks: "What's that?"
Ms Howard answers:
"You can be the teacher
and then you will see."
Lars thinks this is great.
He goes to the teacher's desk
and takes the apples in his hands.
He stands there like an inspector!
Then he asks the teacher:
"I have two apples in my right hand
and three apples in my left hand.
What's that?"
Ms Howard makes a face like a pupil
that doesn't know the answer.

"You . . . have . . . you have . . .
five apples altogether.
Two and three
is the same as one and four.
But what I know for sure is . . ."
She makes this face again like a pupil
that must think about the answer.
The whole class is watching
and waiting.
They all want to hear the answer.
"Well, a pupil with five apples
in his two hands –
what I know for sure is
that he's very, very hungry!"
The children think this is great fun.
This is the best maths class ever.
And they think about new questions:

maths – Mathe

five and three eggs is eight.
And when they all fall down?
Then you have scrambled eggs.
Another one:
there are five flies on the window.
When you catch one, – how many do
you have on the window then?
Not a single one – they all fly away!
Lilli is extremely happy.

scrambled eggs – Rühreier
flies – Fliegen
fly – fliegen

Her magic spells went all wrong,
they weren't helpful at all.
But her teacher has very good ideas
so that nothing is left
from the last spell
(when the other pupils
were very, very strange!).
Lilli watches the inspector.
What's he doing?

His little black book
is still on his desk.

but he isn't writing anymore.
He puts up his hand
because he wants to say something!
Ms Howard says: "Well, Mr Stuart,
what's your question for us?"
But he has no question for the class.
He says: "Well done, Ms Howard.
It was extremely difficult
for you today
but you always know
what to do,
even in the trickiest situations."
Ms Howard is tired but she smiles.
There were so many strange things
today. She wasn't sure
what the inspector would say.
It was a good thing that she
had no idea about Lilli's tricks . . .
Then Ms Howard sends the children

to the playground.
Lilli puts her piece of paper
with the magic spells
into her school bag.
Suddenly she has an idea.
She takes the piece of paper
out again.
She goes out of the classroom
with the other children
and reads her spells once more.
Then she walks to the stairs

(with the others)
and says something very quietly.
She tiptoes back
to the classroom and listens
to the two people in the room.
She hears Ms Howard.
"But Mr Stuart," her teacher says,
"well, this really is a big surprise!"
Lilli takes a quick look.
Mr Stuart is very surprised himself.
He stands there
with flowers in his hands.
He doesn't know what's happening:
"I . . . I just don't know . . . I mean . . .
why . . . suddenly . . . they were
there . . . in my hand . . ."
Ms Howard smiles:

tiptoe – schleichen

"This is so nice of you.
They're beautiful flowers."
Mr Stuart is still very surprised.
"Yes, these flowers . . . I don't understand . . . I mean . . . they were suddenly in my hand . . . in my hand . . . and I don't know . . ."
Ms Howard takes the flowers out of his hand and says:
"We must find a vase for them."
The inspector looks happy now that Ms Howard has the flowers.
How *did* these flowers get there?
Lilli laughs.
"One trick that works!" she says.
She runs down the hall with her piece of paper in her hand.
She will never say magic spells again at school . . . never! . . . never???

Liebe Eltern, liebe Lehrer,

Die meisten Kinder sind sehr stolz darauf, wenn sie ihr erstes Buch in einer fremden Sprache gelesen haben – zu Recht! Mit diesem einfachen und didaktisch aufgearbeiteten englischen *Hexe-Lilli*-Abenteuer können nun sogar schon Englisch-Anfänger begeistert und motiviert werden.
Der Text basiert auf einem Grundwortschatz von ca. 450 Wörtern, was ca. einem Dreivierteljahr Englischunterricht in der fünften Klasse einer weiterführenden Schule entspricht bzw. mit der flächendeckenden Einführung des Grundschulenglisch ca. einem halben Jahr.
Wir haben bei dieser englischen Fas-

sung von *Hexe Lilli* die neuesten Erkenntnisse aus der Fremdsprachendidaktik zu Grunde gelegt.
Bisher ist man im (traditionellen) Fremdsprachenunterricht davon ausgegangen, dass Kinder einen Text in der Fremdsprache nur dann verstehen können, wenn ihnen sämtliche darin enthaltenen grammatischen Strukturen hinlänglich vertraut sind. Wenn Sie dieses Buch durchlesen, wird Ihnen auffallen, dass wir durchaus die Vergangenheit und die Zukunft benutzen oder auch vereinzelt Relativsätze. Dies sind Themen, die nach Lehrplan erst im Laufe der Klasse 6 unterrichtet werden.
Die neueren Forschungen über Verstehensprozesse beim Lesen zeigen jedoch, dass ein Leser (unabhängig vom

Alter) sich vor allem auf die inhaltlichen Informationen und nicht auf die grammatischen Informationen in einem Text konzentriert. Das heißt, in einem Satz wie "An inspector is going to come to our school tomorrow" sind eigentlich nur drei Wörter interessant: inspector – come – school, womit die entscheidenden Informationen genannt sind. Jeder Leser erschließt sich den Sinn ganz leicht selber. Das heißt für den Unterricht oder auch die Lektüre zu Hause, dass Kinder Texte lesen können, die sie inhaltlich verstehen – auch wenn sie die grammatischen Strukturen nicht kennen.

Auf diesen Erkenntnissen beruht der vorliegende Text. Die Sätze haben wir möglichst kurz gehalten, die inhaltlich wichtigen Wörter sind den Kindern

entweder bekannt, können aus dem Deutschen erschlossen werden oder werden erklärt. Auch die Illustrationen haben wir bewusst so ausgewählt, dass sie die Situation nochmals anschaulich darstellen.
Noch ein Wort zu den Vokabel-Erklärungen: Sie sollen Hürden abbauen und nicht neue Hürden schaffen. Deshalb haben wir sie – im Unterschied zu den gängigen Englisch-Lehrwerken – so verfasst, dass sie teilweise aus ganzen Phrasen bestehen und möglichst wenig grammatisches Wissen von den Lesern abverlangen (daher ist z.B. auf die Infinitiv-Form mit "to" verzichtet worden).
Damit Ihr Kind mit seinem ersten englischen *Hexe-Lilli*-Abenteuer zurechtkommt, gehen Sie doch bitte mit ihm

gemeinsam die Lesetipps auf der letzten Seite durch. Jetzt kann eigentlich nichts mehr schief gehen!
Viel Spaß und viel Erfolg bei der Lektüre wünschen

Ellen Butzko und KNISTER

Hexe Lillis ganz geheime Lesetipps:

Wenn du nicht bei jedem Wort weißt, was es heißt, lies einfach weiter. Du wirst merken, die Geschichte verstehst du auch so!

Die Übersetzung von einigen schwierigeren Vokabeln findest du unten auf der jeweiligen Seite. Die übersetzten Vokabeln sind im Text unterstrichen.

Viele englische Wörter, die du noch nicht kennst, sind ganz ähnlich wie im Deutschen. Zum Beispiel idea = Idee, brilliant = brilliant, start = starten, absolutely = absolut.

Manche Wörter wirst du wieder erkennen, weil sie im Deutschen auch verwendet werden. Zum Beispiel: skateboard, sheriff, revolver.

Prima ist, dass du in diesem Buch auch Wörter lernst, die dir deine Englischlehrerin normalerweise nicht beibringt. Zum Beispiel fart = furzen, twit = Dummkopf.

KNISTERnde Spannung

Für den Arena Verlag habe ich inzwischen einen ganzen Stapel spannender Bücher verfaßt:

- **Hexe Lilli**
  Mit vielen Büchern aus der Erfolgsserie
- **Wer verflixt ist Yoko?**
- **Yoko mischt die Schule auf**
- **Yoko und die Gruselnacht im Klassenzimmer**
- **Teppichpiloten**
- **Teppichpiloten starten durch**
- **Teppichpiloten mit Geheimauftrag**
- **Teppichpiloten erobern den Weltraum**
- **Bröselmann und das Steinzeit-Ei**
- **Die Reiter des eisernen Drachen**
- **Willi Wirsing**
- **Alles Spagetti**
- **Wo ist mein Schuh? fragt die Kuh**
- **Knuspermaus im Weihnachtshaus**
- **Nikolauskrimi**

Meine Taschenbücher:

- **Die Sockensuchmaschine**
- **Willi Wirsing**
- **Reiter des eisernen Drachen**
- **Der Krimi vom Weihnachtsmann**

Guten Tag.

Ich bin KNISTER, der die **Hexe Lilli** geschrieben hat. Ich möchte euch gerne mehr über meine Bücher erzählen. Die schreibe ich übrigens mit dem Computer: einem großen, der bei mir zu Hause steht, und einem kleinen auf einem Segelboot.

KNISTER im Internet!
Mit KNISTER Spieleseiten!

Arena

www.knister.de

★ ★KNISTER ★ Jetzt auch im INTERNET! www.knister.de ★

Viel Vergnügen mit der Hexe Lilli!

Hexe Lilli stellt die Schule auf den Kopf

Hexe Lilli macht Zauberquatsch

Hexe Lilli und der Zirkuszauber

Hexe Lilli bei den Piraten

Hexe Lilli und der Weihnachtszauber

Hexe Lilli im Fußballfieber

Arena

★ ★KNISTER ★ Jetzt auch im INTERNET! www.knister.de ★

★ ★ KNISTER ★ ★ Jetzt auch im INTERNET! www.knister.de ★ ★ KNISTER ★ ★ Jetzt auch im INTERNET! www.knister.de ★ ★ KNISTER ★ ★

...noch mehr Abenteuer...

Hexe Lilli wird Detektivin

Hexe Lillis Partyzauber

Hexe Lilli im wilden Wilden Westen

Hexe Lilli und das wilde Indianer-abenteuer

Hexe Lilli und das Geheimnis der Mumie

Hexe Lilli und das Geheimnis der versunkenen Welt

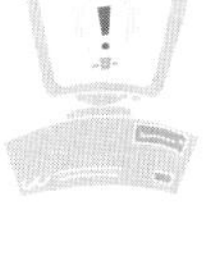

KNISTER
im Internet!
Mit KNISTER
Spieleseiten!

Arena

★ ★ KNISTER ★ ★ Jetzt auch im INTERNET! www.knister.de ★ ★ KNISTER ★ ★ Jetzt auch im INTERNET! www.knister.de ★ ★ KNISTER ★ ★

...und noch mehr von Hexe Lilli

Hexe Lilli und das magische Schwert

Hexe Lilli auf Schloss Dracula

Hexe Lilli und der Vampir mit dem Wackelzahn

Hexe Lilli zaubert Hausaufgaben

Hexe Lilli
Fan-Artikel
(Radiergummis, Stempel, Notizbuch, Computerspiel ...)

Hexe Lilli feiert Geburtstag

☛ Alle **Hexe-Lilli-Geschichten** gibt es auch auf Kassetten.
☞ **Von Europa!**

Arena

★ ★ KNISTER ★ ★ Jetzt auch im INTERNET! www.knister.de ★ ★ KNISTER ★ ★ Jetzt auch im INTERNET! www.knister.de ★ ★ KNISTER ★ ★
★ ★ KNISTER ★ ★ Jetzt auch im INTERNET! www.knister.de ★ ★ KNISTER ★ ★ Jetzt auch im INTERNET! www.knister.de ★ ★ KNISTER ★ ★